NODDY
IN TOYLAND ®

Noddy Goes Vroom!

First published in the UK by HarperCollins Children's Books in 2009

1 3 5 7 9 10 8 6 4 2

ISBN: 978-0-00-731803-2

A CIP catalogue record for this title is available from the British Library.

Printed and bound in China

NODDY
IN TOYLAND®

Noddy Goes Vroom!

HarperCollins *Children's Books*

Noddy loves driving around
Toyland in his red and yellow car.
He likes to keep it clean and shiny.

Look, Noddy's giving you a cheery wave.
Can you wave back?

Noddy has lots of
adventures in his little car.
Here he is, driving through the
lovely, green countryside.

Make sure you don't
go too fast, Noddy!

And here's Noddy in his
car singing a happy little song.

What's your favourite
song? Can you sing
it for Noddy?

Look, here's Noddy flying
his plane high in the sky.
It's the same colour as his
car and just as shiny.

Can you guess
what Noddy's about
to do next?

Clever Noddy has used the smoke trails from his plane to draw a shape in the sky.

Can you tell what it is?

Noddy's friends like
to go vroom too! Here he is,
driving alongside Tessie Bear.

Tessie Bear's car is quite different
from Noddy's. Can you say how?

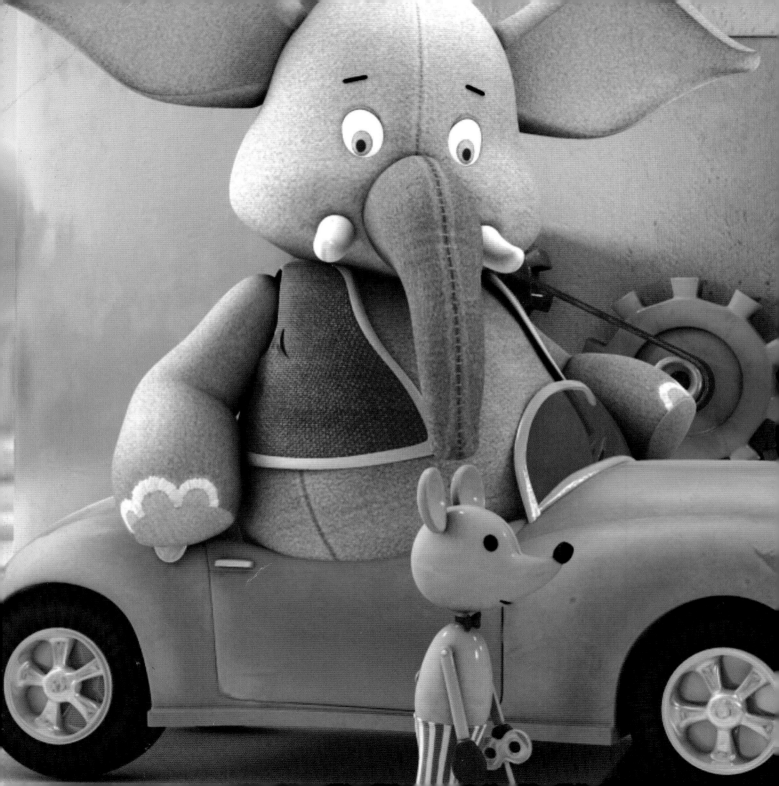

Noddy's friend Jumbo has a car too, but he can only just fit inside!

Be careful you don't get stuck, Jumbo!

What's Noddy's friend Lindy up to? It looks like she's painting Noddy's little car!

Do you think
Noddy
will like it?

Now, what's this bobbing
up and down in the water?

Can you show us, Noddy?

It's a Jet Ski!

Noddy looks like he's having lots
of fun zooming along.
Poor Bumpy Dog isn't quite so sure!

Can you see something
up there in the sky?
It's Noddy in his helicopter!

He looks very small because
he's flying so high!

Look, Noddy's about to
land his helicopter.
Go steady, Noddy!

Do you think Bumpy Dog
enjoyed the flight?

NODDY
IN TOYLAND®

**Look out for more
Noddy in Toyland books!**

NODDY
IN TOYLAND

Hide-and-Seek Fun

NODDY
IN TOYLAND

Noddy and the Pirates